Old MacDonald
Had a Farm

Thanks to John and Beth Thorold

Library of Congress Catalog Number: 80-81329

ISBN 0-675-01065-9

Published by
TRADE DIVISION
Charles E. Merrill Publishing Company
A Bell & Howell Company
Columbus, Ohio 43216

Old MacDonald
Had a Farm

Illustrated
by
David Frankland

Old MacDonald Had a Farm

Old MacDonald had a farm,
Ee-ay, ee-ay, oh !
And on that farm
He had some cows,
Ee-ay, ee-ay, oh !

With a moo-moo here,
And a moo-moo there,
Here a moo,
There a moo,
Ev'rywhere a moo-moo.

Old MacDonald had a farm,
Ee-ay, ee-ay, oh !

Old MacDonald had a farm,
Ee-ay, ee-ay, oh!
And on that farm
He had a pig,
Ee-ay, ee-ay, oh!

With an oink-oink here,
And an oink-oink there,
Here an oink,
There an oink,
Ev'rywhere an oink-oink.

With a moo-moo here,
And a moo-moo there,
Here a moo,
There a moo,
Ev'rywhere a moo-moo. . .

Old MacDonald had a farm,
Ee-ay, ee-ay, oh!
And on that farm
He had a rooster,
Ee-ay, ee-ay, oh!

With a cock-a-doodle here,
And a cock-a-doodle there,
Here a doodle,
There a doodle,
Ev'rywhere a cock-a-doodle.

With an oink-oink here,
And an oink-oink there,
Here an oink,
There an oink,
Ev'rywhere an oink-oink. . .

Old MacDonald had a farm,
Ee-ay, ee-ay, oh!
And on that farm
He had some sheep,
Ee-ay, ee-ay, oh!

With a baa-baa here,
And a baa-baa there,
Here a baa,
There a baa,
Ev'rywhere a baa-baa.

With a cock-a-doodle here,
And a cock-a-doodle there,
Here a doodle,
There a doodle,
Ev'rywhere a cock-a-doodle. . .

Old MacDonald had a farm,
Ee-ay, ee-ay, oh!
And on that farm
He had a dog,
Ee-ay, ee-ay, oh!

With a woof-woof here,
And a woof-woof there,
Here a woof,
There a woof,
Ev'rywhere a woof-woof.

With a baa-baa here,
And a baa-baa there,
Here a baa,
There a baa,
Ev'rywhere a baa-baa...

Old MacDonald had a farm,
Ee-ay, ee-ay, oh!
And on that farm
He had a turkey,
Ee-ay, ee-ay, oh!

With a gobble-gobble here,
And a gobble-gobble there,
Here a gobble,
There a gobble,
Ev'rywhere a gobble-gobble.

With a woof-woof here,
And a woof-woof there,
Here a woof,
There a woof,
Ev'rywhere a woof-woof. . .

Old MacDonald had a farm,
Ee-ay, ee-ay, oh!
And on that farm
He had a horse,
Ee-ay, ee-ay, oh!

With a neigh-neigh here,
And a neigh-neigh there,
Here a neigh,
There a neigh,
Ev'rywhere a neigh-neigh.

With a gobble-gobble here,
And a gobble-gobble there,
Here a gobble,
There a gobble,
Ev'rywhere a gobble-gobble. . .

18

Old MacDonald had a farm,
Ee-ay, ee-ay, oh!
And on that farm
He had some ducks,
Ee-ay, ee-ay, oh!

With a quack-quack here,
And a quack-quack there,
Here a quack,
There a quack,
Ev'rywhere a quack-quack.

With a neigh-neigh here,
And a neigh-neigh there,
Here a neigh,
There a neigh,
Ev'rywhere a neigh-neigh. . .

Old MacDonald had a farm,
Ee-ay, ee-ay, oh!
And on that farm
He had a cat,
Ee-ay, ee-ay, oh!

With a meow-meow here,
And a meow-meow there,
Here a meow,
There a meow,
Ev'rywhere a meow-meow.

With a quack-quack here,
And a quack-quack there,
Here a quack,
There a quack,
Ev'rywhere a quack-quack. . .

Old MacDonald had a farm,
Ee-ay, ee-ay, oh!
And on that farm
He had some crows,
Ee-ay, ee-ay, oh!

With a caw-caw here,
And a caw-caw there,
Here a caw,
There a caw,
Ev'rywhere a caw-caw.

With a meow-meow here,
And a meow-meow there,
Here a meow,
There a meow,
Ev'rywhere a meow-meow. . .

24

Old MacDonald had a farm,
Ee-ay, ee-ay, oh!
And on that farm
He had some frogs,
Ee-ay, ee-ay, oh!

With a croak-croak here,
And a croak-croak there,
Here a croak,
There a croak,
Ev'rywhere a croak-croak.

With a caw-caw here,
And a caw-caw there,
Here a caw,
There a caw,
Ev'rywhere a caw-caw. . .

Old MacDonald had a farm,
Ee-ay, ee-ay, oh!
And on that farm
He had some hens,
Ee-ay, ee-ay, oh!

With a cluck-cluck here,
And a cluck-cluck there,
Here a cluck,
There a cluck,
Ev'rywhere a cluck-cluck.

With a croak-croak here,
And a croak-croak there,
Here a croak,
There a croak,
Ev'rywhere a croak-croak. . .

The End